The HALL of BEASTS

The HALL of BEASTS

Written and Illustrated by
MARK SHASHA

Simon & Schuster Books for Young Readers

SIMON & SCHUSTER BOOKS FOR YOUNG READERS
An imprint of Simon & Schuster Children's Publishing Division
1230 Avenue of the Americas
New York, NY 10020
Copyright © 1994 by Mark Sasha

Simon & Schuster Books for Young Readers
is a trademark of Simon & Schuster
Designed by Paul Zakris
The text of this book was set in 14 point Goudy.
The illustrations were done in pastels.
Manufactured in the United States of America 10 9 8 7 6 5 4 3 2

Library of Congress Cataloging-in-Publication Data
Shasha, Mark.
The Hall of Beasts / by Mark Shasha p. cm.
Summary: Grandpa tells a story about a wonderful painting of animals on the
walls of a room in an inn, which come to life and leave the walls.
[1. Art—Fiction.   2. Animals—Fiction.   3. Grandfathers—Fiction.]   I. Title.
PZ7.S5324Hal   1993   [E]—dc20   92-39520   CIP
ISBN: 0-671-79893-6

With love to Danuta
—M.S.

Special thanks to Sarah, Emily, Pam and Lucille

It would be a while before the family sat down to eat, so the old man took his granddaughter's hand and led her away from the gathering.

"There's something I want to show you, Jennie," he said, pointing across a lonely stretch of beach to a building in the distance.

Jennie squinted into the salty wind. "A house, Grandpa?" she said.

Her grandpa bent to whisper in her ear. "Animals!" he said.

Jennie's eyes opened wide in excitement. She loved animals. "Let's go!" Jennie said.

They headed across the beach toward the point.

"It's an old inn," Grandpa said, "once owned by a sea captain. When I was little, I stayed there with my grandfather. One great room had walls covered with a marvelous painting of animals. It was called the Hall of Beasts.

"I asked the captain how the animals had gotten there. He told me that one day a mysterious man had come looking for a room but had no money. He offered instead to paint the ballroom in return for a place to stay.

"The sea captain accepted the offer, but then the man said there was something the captain should know. 'The animals must never be abandoned,' he said, 'or they will vanish at the first light of day.' The captain agreed to respect the painter's wishes.

"When the painting was finished, it was called a great masterpiece. The animals were so lifelike that visitors were breathless at the first sight of them.

"The inn became famous for its extraordinary mural."

As they neared the inn, Jennie could see
plainly that the place was run-down. Grandpa
told her how, for many years, the inn had been
neglected. The roof began to leak and the wood
began to rot. The captain then decided to close
the inn so it could be repaired. Soon people
began to forget about the Hall of Beasts.

Jennie and her grandpa reached the old inn.
"I'm afraid that tomorrow this building will
be torn down," said Grandpa.
He took Jennie's hand and led her inside
carefully.
Slowly, they climbed the stairs.

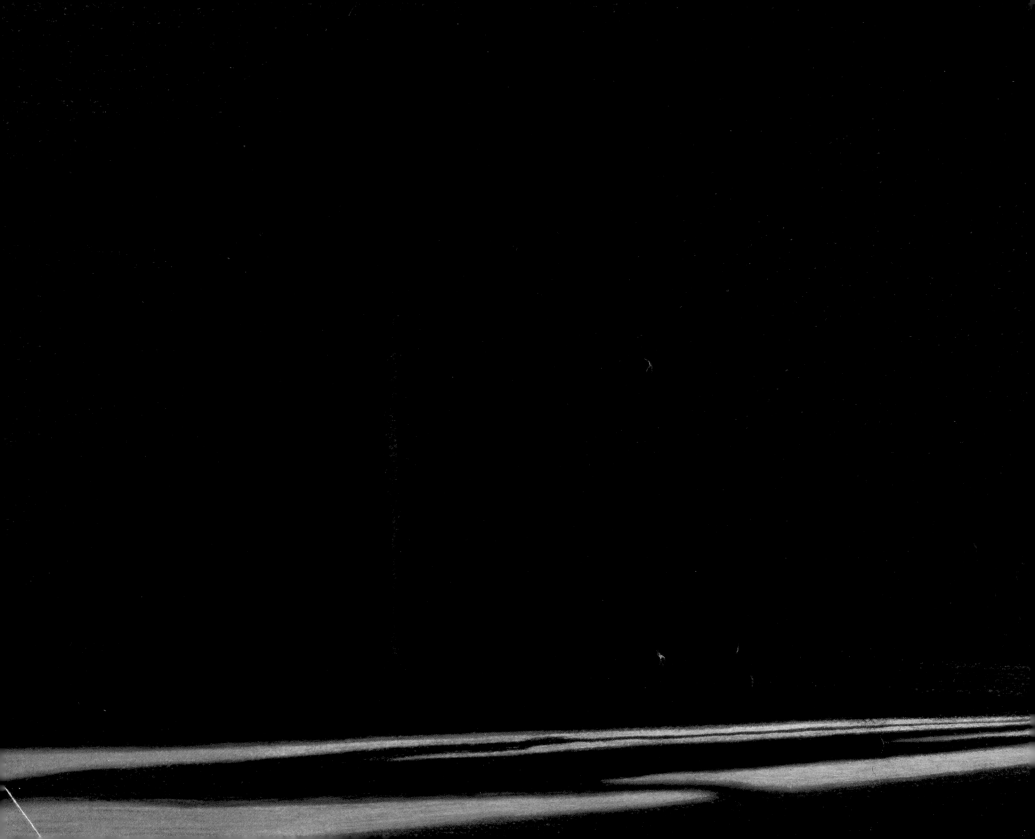

Grandpa opened a pair of heavy doors. The room was completely dark.

"Grandpa, I can't see anything," Jennie said.

"I'm sure this is the Hall of Beasts," Grandpa whispered.

The air was musty and thick.
There was just enough light
from the open doors for
Grandpa to find the heavy
curtains that covered the windows.
He pulled them aside and light
flooded the great hall.

"Look," cried Jennie.

"Yes!" Grandpa said. "Exactly as I..."

Jennie gasped, pointing to a rabbit that hopped from the wall and scurried past them.

"Grandpa, the animals are leaving the wall!"

A sea gull swooped overhead! More rabbits hopped by. Then another gull—and another circled the room.

Hooves hit the floor as a deer fled past.
Grandpa scooped up Jennie as more animals
bolted for the door.

Out they rushed—down the stairs, out the
door, and across the grassy dunes.

Suddenly, the walls were empty.

Jennie and her grandfather could hardly
believe what they had seen. Grandpa told Jennie
he was certain the animals had returned to some
magical place where the painter had first
encountered them.

But Jennie was not so sure.